The Full Monty

WENDY HOLDEN
Based on the screenplay by
SIMON BEAUFOY

Level 4

Retold by Anne Collins
Series Editors: Andy Hopkins and Jocelyn Potter

Pearson Education Limited
Edinburgh Gate, Harlow,
Essex CM20 2JE, England
and Associated Companies throughout the world.

ISBN 0 582 41981 6

First published in Great Britain by HarperCollins Publishers Ltd 1998
This edition first published 1999

Third impression 2001

Copyright © Twentieth Century Fox Film Corporation 1998, 1999
Cover art and photographs courtesy of Fox Searchlight
All rights reserved

Typeset by Digital Type, London
Set in 11/13pt Bembo
Printed in Spain by Mateu Cromo, S.A. Pinto (Madrid)

Published by Pearson Education Limited in association with
Penguin Books Ltd, both companies being subsidiaries of Pearson Plc

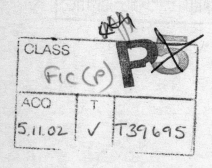

For a complete list of the titles available in the Penguin Readers series please write to your local
Pearson Education office or to: Marketing Department, Penguin Longman Publishing,
5 Bentinck Street, London W1M 5RN.

Introduction

Sheryl and Louise couldn't believe their ears. They stared at Gaz. 'All the way?' Sheryl repeated. 'Everything? Do you mean ... the full monty? You?'

'Yes,' Gaz said proudly.

Gaz, an unemployed steel factory worker, needs a large sum of money quickly so he can continue seeing his son, Nathan. Gaz has had many crazy ideas in his life, but his plan to get this money seems the craziest of all. Or is it?

Gaz and five equally unlikely men decide to copy the popular American male strippers' group, the Chippendales, by forming their own strippers' group. None of the men has had any experience of taking their clothes off in public. They include Dave, very worried about his weight; Lomper, lonely and depressed; and Gerald, who still hasn't dared to tell his wife that he lost his job six months ago. But to make sure the local women come to the show, Gaz knows his group must be *better* than the Chippendales. To the horror of the others, he tells the women that the group will take *all* their clothes off. The men refuse – they do not want to do the show. But will these six unlikely strippers change their minds and dare to go for the 'full monty'?

The Full Monty is a very popular film, starring Robert Carlyle as Gaz. It is very funny, but has a serious side too. It is a story of modern times – a story of ordinary men who have been unemployed for a long time and feel that society does not need them any more. But, above all, it is a film about changing direction, finding new friends and making a new start.

Contents

Chapter 1   The Chippendales Come to Sheffield

Twenty-five years ago, the city of Sheffield in the north of England was a wonderful and exciting place to live. In those days, Sheffield produced the world's finest steel, and steel was big business. More than a hundred thousand men worked night and day in the great steel factories, making everything from steel girders to knives and forks.

There was plenty of work and plenty of money. The people of Sheffield worked hard, but they also enjoyed spending the money they earned. They went out at night to pubs and restaurants and took their families on holiday every year. Life was very good.

But within a few short years, everything changed. Sheffield began to face competition from steel factories in other parts of the world. The Far East could produce steel more cheaply than Sheffield and, one by one, the great steel factories of Sheffield closed.

The men who had worked all their lives in the steel factories lost their jobs. They had no money to spend, nothing to do and nowhere to go except the local Job Club. Now it was the women who had to find work to support their families. So they found jobs in local shops and businesses. The pay was not as good as the men had earned in the steel factories, but it was something. And they were earning money while their husbands sat at home.

◆

One cold Sunday afternoon in April, two men and a boy – Gary (Gaz) Schofield, Dave Horsfall and Gaz's twelve-year-old son, Nathan – were walking through an empty steel factory. Dave was carrying a steel girder on his shoulder.

Gaz was walking ahead with Nathan. He was wearing his usual jeans, T-shirt and black leather jacket. He was thirty-eight and unemployed. Two years ago his wife, Mandy, had left him and she was now living with another man.

'Who's going to want this old girder, then?' complained Dave. He wasn't in a very good mood. The girder was heavy and difficult to carry. Gaz had arrived at his house an hour ago with the idea of going to the factory and stealing a girder. They could sell it and make a bit of money, Gaz said. As usual, Dave had agreed to do what he wanted. So now here they were in the factory, and Dave was doing all the work.

Nathan wasn't happy either. 'This is stealing, Dad,' he said. 'What will happen if we're caught?'

Gaz looked down into his son's face, but Nathan knew that Gaz wasn't really listening to him.

'Of course it isn't stealing, Nathan,' he said. 'Just don't tell your Mum, that's all.' Then he added, 'Ten years we worked in here. Now look.'

The great empty factory had pools of water on the floor and was full of broken machinery. Gaz and Dave had both started working there when they were young men. Gaz could still hear the noise of the great machines and feel the heat from the enormous fires on his face. A thousand men had worked in the factory but now only their ghosts were left.

2

They had reached the large metal doorway of the factory. Dave was red in the face from carrying the heavy girder. He was glad to get out into the fresh air. It made him sad to remember the good days when he and Gaz had worked together in the factory. It had closed down three years ago and they had been out of work since then.

'Hey, listen,' Dave said suddenly. 'What's that noise? It sounds like music.'

The sounds came closer and closer. Now they could clearly hear a drum. Suddenly, round the corner marched a group of twenty men and women, all playing musical instruments. The last musician in the group was a tall, thin red-haired man, playing a cornet.

'It's the factory band,' explained Nathan. 'They still play, you know.'

'Quick!' said Gaz. 'Hide!'

In his terror Dave dropped the girder, which fell to the ground with a crash. Gaz, Dave and Nathan hid behind the door while the band passed. Suddenly, the red-haired man left the group and ran back towards the factory.

'It's Lomper, the security guard,' warned Dave.

Lomper had noticed that the door of the factory was open. He closed it, locking it with his key. Now Gaz, Dave and Nathan were locked inside. There was no escape.

Dave and Nathan looked at Gaz.

'Now what do we do?' asked Nathan. 'How do we get out of here?' His father's plans always went wrong.

But Gaz wasn't worried. 'It's all right,' he told them. 'I've got an idea.'

◆

Fifteen minutes later, Gaz, Dave and Nathan were standing on top of an old car in the dirty black water of the canal which ran along by the factory. They had taken not one girder, but two, pulled them through a broken window and carried them to the canal.

The canal was too wide to cross, but they had seen the old car in the middle. They had reached the roof of the car by placing one girder from the canal bank to the car and walking across it as a bridge. Then they had placed the other girder from the car's roof to the far bank, and intended to walk across that too.

Nathan, the smallest and lightest, ran quickly across the girder and reached the other canal bank safely. He turned and faced his father.

'Can't we do normal things sometimes, Dad?' he asked unhappily.

He thought about all his school friends, sitting at home playing computer games or watching football with their fathers. Why couldn't he and Gaz do the same? But Gaz, as usual, had an answer. He smiled at his son and replied, 'What's the matter with you, Nathan? This *is* normal. Now pick up the girder and pull it across.'

Nathan managed to lift the girder a little, but it was too heavy for him. It fell out of his hands and disappeared into the cold black water.

'Oh, Nathan!' said Gaz. 'That's twenty pounds we've lost.' Nathan looked hurt and upset and began to walk away. He had tried to help.

Gaz and Dave were still standing on the roof of the car. Every time they moved, the car moved too, sinking deeper into the mud at the bottom of the canal. Dave pointed to the dirty water in terror. 'Gaz! This car is sinking!'

For the hundredth time that afternoon, he asked himself why he had agreed to help Gaz steal the girder. It was just another of Gaz's stupid ideas and his ideas always ended badly. Not badly for Gaz, but badly for Dave. Well, this really was the last time. He was never going to listen to Gaz again.

Gaz and Dave were still standing on the roof of the car.

Gaz stepped down on to the front of the car, looking after Nathan and calling his name. The car moved dangerously, and the other girder, still on the roof, fell off into the water. Their last chance of a dry escape had gone.

'Great, Gaz!' said Dave. 'What are we going to do now?'

Gaz pushed his hands through his hair. 'I don't know,' he said finally, and Dave knew that all was lost.

◆

It was getting dark. Gaz, Dave and Nathan were walking down some steep steps near the canal. They were on their way home at last.

Dave was very cold in his wet clothes. Every time he took a step, the dirty water from the canal ran down his legs and into his shoes.

Gaz, on the other hand, was completely dry. He had taken off his clothes and held them high and dry above his head while he walked naked across the canal. He laughed to himself as he remembered Dave falling into the water.

'Why didn't you take your clothes off, too?' he asked.

'Oh, shut up, Gaz,' said Dave.

Dave was very embarrassed about his body. He knew he ate too much and was too fat. Dave had always been fat, but when he was working, he did a lot of exercise and so he lost weight. These days he did no exercise and couldn't lose any weight. He hated his body and sometimes he hated himself.

They crossed the street at the bottom of the steps and turned the corner. Then they stopped in surprise. A most unusual sight was in front of them.

Outside the Millthorpe Working Men's Club stood a line of women, all dressed in their best clothes. They were clearly waiting for something to happen. From inside the Club came the sound of loud music.

'What's all this, then?' asked Gaz.

Nathan already knew the answer. He had heard his mother talking excitedly about it to a friend on the phone.

'It's the Chippendales,' he replied. 'You know. That American group of male strippers.'

'Male strippers?' asked Gaz. He stared at his son, unable to believe his ears.

'Yes,' said Nathan. 'Look, there's a photograph.'

On the wall of the Working Men's Club there was a full colour photograph of the Chippendales. They were very handsome, and naked from the waist up. The words 'For One Night, Women Only' and 'The Men Are Here' were written in large red letters across the photograph. Gaz stared at the photograph and his face grew dark with anger.

'Women only?' he said. 'But this is a Working *Men's* Club. Who do they think they are, these Chippendales? I don't think much of them at all. They've got nothing to be proud of. What woman would pay money to see *them*?'

Dave looked sadly away down the street. 'My wife would,' he said quietly.

'Jean?' said Gaz. 'You mean, Jean … *Jean's* in there?'

'Yes,' said Dave unhappily. 'With two of her friends. Well, it's her money, isn't it?' This was exactly what Jean had said to him the night before. And he knew she was right. She had a good job in a local shop and she could spend her money any way she wanted.

But Gaz hadn't finished yet. 'Well that's terrible, Dave,' he said. 'There's only one thing to do. We'll have to go in there and get Jean out. Come on, you two. Don't just stand there.'

Nathan and Dave turned pale. Another of Gaz's crazy ideas! And this one was sure to get them all into trouble.

'You can't, Dad,' said Nathan. 'It says "Women Only".'

But it was too late. Gaz wasn't listening. He was already walking towards the window of the men's toilet.

Chapter 2   At the Job Club

A few minutes later, Nathan dropped on to the floor of the men's toilet from the narrow window high up in the wall. Gaz followed him, resting his foot on his son's shoulder to help himself down. Dave was too large to fit through the window and had to wait outside in the street.

'Just hurry, will you?' called Dave. 'My feet are freezing.'

'You really should be more grateful, Dave,' replied Gaz. 'We're doing this for *you* – going into this awful place to get Jean out.'

Dave knew this wasn't true. He hadn't wanted to break into the Club and get Jean out at all.

7

Nathan didn't say anything. He was thirsty, hungry and ready for bed. What were they doing in a place like this on a Sunday night? Had Gaz forgotten that tomorrow was a school day?

Loud music was coming from inside the Club. Gaz put his hands on his son's shoulders and said, 'Right, then, I'll wait here. You find Jean and tell her Dave wants to speak to her outside, all right?'

'Dad, do I have to?' asked Nathan. He was afraid of Jean. What would she say when she saw a twelve-year-old boy here? But Gaz had decided and Nathan knew he had no choice. Gaz was already opening the heavy main door of the toilet, ready to push Nathan out into the Club.

The noise of the music and the heat from the Club hit Gaz and Nathan in the face. The room was in half darkness and for a moment it was difficult to see anything. But the stage was brightly lit. Gaz and Nathan looked towards it and their mouths fell open in astonishment.

The Chippendales were in the middle of their performance. They were dancing and moving their half-naked bodies sexily in time to the music. All the women who had been standing quietly in a queue outside the Club were crowding round. But they weren't quiet now.

Hundreds of women – housewives and mothers, women who worked in shops and banks, young girls and old grandmothers – were climbing excitedly over each other and pushing each other out of the way. They all wanted to get as near as possible to the half-naked men on the stage. They watched the Chippendales dancing and taking off their clothes, and shouted as loudly as they could, 'Off! Off! Off!' They were loving every minute of the show.

Gaz had never seen anything like it in all his life. For a few minutes he couldn't say anything. Then, still staring at the women, he pushed Nathan forwards into the darkness.

Suddenly, he saw three women coming straight towards him as they walked towards the men's toilet. One of them had short hair and a shiny pink face and was wearing a very short skirt. It was Jean with two friends, Sharon and Bee.

Quickly, Gaz ran back and hid inside one of the toilets, shutting the door behind him. Through a small hole in the door, he saw the three women come in, laughing and joking loudly. They were clearly having a very good time.

'I'm not waiting in that queue,' said Jean, talking about the long line of women waiting for the ladies' toilet. The three women went to the toilet and then stood in front of the mirror, combing their hair and putting on their make-up. From his hiding place, Gaz could hear every word of their conversation. They were talking about Frankie, a young man who worked in the same shop as Jean. Jean's two friends started to make jokes about Frankie.

'Frankie really likes you, you know,' said Sharon.

'No, he doesn't,' said Jean, starting to get a little angry. Then her voice changed and she said softly, 'But even if he did, I couldn't do anything to hurt Dave. Not even if I wanted to.' She looked up at her two friends standing behind her and suddenly her eyes filled with tears. 'But . . . you know, Dave's almost given up. He's lost interest in everything. He's given up trying to find a job . . . and he's just not interested in me any more.'

Sharon and Bee were sorry they had made jokes about Frankie. They knew Jean still loved Dave and that she was having a difficult time at home. Since he had become unemployed, Dave had become more and more depressed, and now he was beginning to pull Jean down with him.

'Don't worry, Jean,' said Bee. 'Things will get better, you'll see.' Jean managed a smile and the three of them went back into the Club. After waiting for a few minutes to make sure they had gone, Gaz came out of the toilet.

Suddenly, Dave's head appeared at the window and his voice called sadly, 'Gaz, Gaz. That was Jean, wasn't it?'

Dave had heard some, but not all, of the women's conversation. He thought he had heard Jean talking about a man at work who liked her.

'No, no, it wasn't Jean, Dave,' Gaz lied. He had suddenly lost all interest in adventure. 'I'm going back into the Club to get Nathan,' he said.

Nathan was sitting alone at a small table, still staring at the stage. Gaz realized that the women were too busy having fun to notice him. He walked over to Nathan and pulled him to his feet. 'Come on, Nathan,' he said. 'We're going home.'

The Chippendales had reached the final part of their act. They stood at the front of the stage, almost completely naked now. They were smiling and holding out their arms to the crowd, inviting them to come up to the stage. To Gaz's astonishment, he saw women run up to the Chippendales and give them five and ten pound notes.

'What about Jean?' asked Nathan.

Gaz saw Jean on her feet, dancing and singing. 'Jean's busy,' he replied sadly, pulling Nathan back towards the men's toilets and their escape route.

◆

The next morning, Monday, Nathan was back at school and Gaz and Dave were sitting at a table in the local Job Club. With them were twenty or so other unemployed men from the steel factory.

The Job Club wasn't a very cheerful or pleasant place. Many of the men had been unemployed for a long time, and the Job Club didn't give them much hope. The dirty walls were covered with red and white notices, informing people how to get jobs. But everyone in the room knew there were very few jobs around.

Many men had become depressed and felt there was no reason to go to the Job Club.

Gaz and Dave went there three or four times a week. They went mainly to see their friends and for the free cup of coffee and the chance to get warm.

The manager of the Job Club, Luke Marcus, was telling the men how to write application letters. It was his job to try and get them back to work. He knew he was wasting his time with most of them and that they were just waiting for him to go away. Most of them had given up hope of ever finding another job. But there were one or two older men in the room who still listened to Luke, and he wanted to help them as much as he could.

'Right, I want you to finish your letters by the time I get back,' he said. 'If you have any problems, I'm in my office.' He went out and closed the door behind him.

As soon as the door had shut, the men reached under the tables and got out newspapers, cigarettes and packs of cards. Some of them made paper aeroplanes out of the paper for their application letters.

Gaz sat with a cigarette between his fingers. He was still thinking about the women at the Chippendales' show, and his thoughts weren't happy ones.

'Women don't need men any more,' he said to Dave and anyone else who wanted to listen. 'We're useless. A few more years and we won't exist. Except in a zoo or something. We'll be finished. Yesterday's news.'

An older man in his fifties was sitting at a computer, trying to write a job application. This was Gerald Cooper, who had been Gaz's and Dave's boss at the steel factory.

'Shut up!' said Gerald sharply. 'Some of us are trying to get a job.' He looked at Gaz's cigarette and then at the sign above their heads. 'Hey! Can't you read? It says "No Smoking" in here.'

Gaz sat back in his seat with his cigarette still in his hand, not intending to put it out.

'Yes, and it says "Job Club" too,' he said. 'When was the last time you saw a job in here?' The men sitting around him began to laugh. 'You forget, Gerald,' Gaz went on, 'you're not our boss any more. You're just like the rest of us – finished.'

Gerald turned to Gaz with an angry fire in his eyes, but all he said again was, 'Shut up!'

Dave was still thinking about the Chippendales. 'How many women were there?' he asked Gaz.

'About a thousand,' Gaz guessed.

'Well, if each of those women paid ten pounds, that's ten pounds by a thousand ...' Dave started to count on his fingers, but the sum was too difficult for him. 'That's well ... er ... that's a lot of money.'

'Ten thousand pounds,' said another man helpfully.

'How much?' asked Gaz quietly. Suddenly, everyone in the room stopped what they were doing and listened.

'Ten thousand pounds,' repeated the man.

Gaz stared at Dave. 'Well,' he said, 'that's an interesting thought, isn't it?' He had a strange look on his face, a look which Dave didn't like at all. He had seen that look many times before and he knew it meant trouble. It was the look Gaz had when he was getting one of his crazy ideas.

Chapter 3   Lomper

A few days later, Gaz and Dave were out running on the high ground above Sheffield. The city was spread out below them like an enormous blanket, and in the distance, they saw the busy motorway with cars rushing up and down to London.

Dave wasn't enjoying the run at all. They were going up a

steep hill and he was getting more and more red in the face, and finding it difficult to breathe.

Gaz was running easily up the hill several steps ahead of Dave. He was thinking about Nathan's mother, Mandy. He had gone round to see her the night before. Mandy lived with her boyfriend, Barry, in Barry's house. Barry had a good job in computers and his house was modern, warm and comfortable – not cold and untidy like Gaz's small flat.

For most of the time, Nathan lived with Mandy and Barry, but for two days a week he was allowed to stay with Gaz. Now, though, perhaps everything was going to change.

Gaz was supposed to pay Mandy some money every month to help her buy things for Nathan. But for a long time, he hadn't been able to afford to pay her. Gaz was unemployed and received only a very small amount of money from the government every week.

Mandy was now waiting for seven hundred pounds from him, and last week he had received a letter from the court, ordering him to pay it. If he didn't, said the letter, he wouldn't be able to spend time with Nathan any more. The boy would live with Mandy and Barry all the time, and Gaz wouldn't be allowed to see him.

This was very serious for Gaz. He loved Nathan more than anything in the world and would do anything to continue seeing him. So he had gone to see Mandy, to explain that he really didn't have the money.

But Mandy refused to listen, and then, to make everything worse, her boyfriend, Barry, had appeared. It was two years since Mandy had moved in with Barry, but Gaz still hadn't got used to the idea. He didn't like Barry and thought he was boring. But at the same time he was jealous of Barry's nice house, good job and new car. All the things Gaz wanted to give Mandy and Nathan, but couldn't.

13

Barry also had a good relationship with Nathan, and Gaz didn't like that. Barry took an interest in the boy, bought him nice presents and was planning to take him to EuroDisney.

'Nathan's yours and mine,' Gaz had shouted at Mandy, pointing angrily to Barry. 'Not his!'

'Fine, Gaz,' she had replied. 'You can go off and play your games if you want to. But in future, Nathan's going to have two good parents.'

Mandy had had tears in her eyes and her face was full of pain. She knew how much Gaz loved his son, but at the same time she was afraid – afraid he could lead Nathan into trouble. Nathan had a better chance with Barry as a parent.

Barry had just smiled and pulled Mandy inside. 'Good night, Gary,' he had said, closing the door in Gaz's face.

So Gaz had to find seven hundred pounds to pay Mandy, or lose Nathan. And he couldn't live with the thought of not seeing his son any more.

♦

Gaz could think of only one way to get such a large sum of money quickly, but he needed Dave's help. And every time he tried to talk to Dave about it, Dave refused to listen.

'No, Gaz,' he said. 'I'm not stripping like the Chippendales. I'm not taking my clothes off for anybody.'

'But, Dave . . . Nathan's my kid. He's all I have and I'll lose him if I can't find the money,' said Gaz.

'No,' said Dave again. 'No, no, no.'

Gaz was silent for a few minutes. Then he said, 'Well, I suppose I could start stealing cars again.'

Dave looked at Gaz in horror. A few years ago, Gaz had needed money to buy things for Mandy and Nathan. So he had stolen a car, been caught by the police and ended up in prison. While he was there, Mandy had met Barry and got herself a good job in a clothes factory. When Gaz came out of prison, she didn't want to know him. Soon afterwards, she moved in with Barry.

Dave remembered the terrible time Gaz had had in prison. He didn't want it to happen again, so he said, 'All right, Gaz, all right. You win. I'll help you.'

But Gaz was running ahead up the hill and didn't hear. Dave was very tired and had a bad headache. He dropped to his hands and knees on the ground and closed his eyes with the pain. Then he heard a noise – the sound of someone trying to start a car. He opened his eyes again.

A dirty old car was parked further up the hill. Dave was very pleased to have a reason to stop running. He walked up to the car and asked the driver, 'Do you want any help?'

Without waiting for an answer, he looked inside the engine of the car. Dave knew a lot about cars and he saw at once what the problem was – one of the leads was dirty. He took out the lead, cleaned it on his T-shirt and placed it back inside the engine.

'Try it again now,' he said to the driver.

The man turned the key and the engine started immediately. Dave walked up to the driver's window and looked at the man inside. To his surprise, he recognized Lomper, the red-haired security guard from the steel factory who had been playing his cornet in the band. Lomper's face was pale and he seemed very nervous.

'Didn't you work up at the steel factory before it closed?' asked Dave.

Lomper stared straight ahead. He didn't speak at all – not even to thank Dave for fixing his car. Dave rested against the car, not noticing the strange smell of smoke or the tube that led into the car from the pipe at the back. The car slowly began to fill with smoke.

'I thought I knew you,' continued Dave. He was in the mood

15

for talking. 'I used to work at the factory too, with Gaz.' Still Lomper didn't reply. 'Have you got any work?'

Lomper shook his head unhappily. Dave knew his security guard job could only be part-time. 'No, well, there's not a lot of it about, is there?' said Dave. Still Lomper said nothing. The air around him became thick with smoke.

Dave was getting angry at Lomper's silence. 'All right, then, don't thank me,' he said, and started to walk up the hill. Gaz was waiting at the top, smoking a cigarette and looking down into the valley. As Dave came nearer, Gaz lit another cigarette and held it out to his friend.

But Dave was thinking hard. Something was wrong – something was very wrong – with the man in the car. But what was it? What was it?

He had almost reached Gaz when he realized. He stopped, turned and ran back down the hill as fast as he could. Gaz stood in astonishment, still holding out the cigarette. He had never seen Dave move so quickly.

'Dave?' he called.

But Dave was already at the car. He opened the door and pulled Lomper out, followed by a great cloud of smoke. Lomper lay on his back on the ground, coughing loudly.

'Are you all right?' asked Dave anxiously.

Lomper opened his eyes. He saw a large man bending over him – the same man who had fixed his car engine and had now stopped him from killing himself. And he had wanted to die.

'You fool!' was all he said.

Dave couldn't believe his ears. Instead of being grateful, Lomper was angry with him. Without a word, he reached down and pulled Lomper up. Before Lomper knew what was happening, Dave had pushed him back into the smoke-filled car and shut the door. He took no notice of Lomper knocking on the window from inside.

Lomper lay on his back on the ground, coughing loudly. 'Are you all right?' asked Dave anxiously.

◆

An hour later, Lomper was sitting with Gaz and Dave in the long grass at the top of the hill. They were smoking and talking about the best way for Lomper to kill himself.

'You could shoot yourself,' suggested Dave, trying to be helpful.

'That's no good,' said Gaz. 'Where's he going to get a gun from round here?' Even Gaz didn't know anyone with a gun. 'You could find yourself a high bridge,' he added.

Lomper shook his head. 'I don't like heights,' he said.

'Well, then,' said Dave brightly. 'Jump in the river.'

Lomper was silent for a moment. But then he said, 'I can't swim.'

'You don't *have to* swim, you fool,' said Gaz. 'You're not very enthusiastic, are you?'

Lomper looked down, ashamed.

'Sorry,' he said. It was the sixteenth time he had said he was sorry that hour.

'I know,' said Dave. 'You could stand in the middle of the road and get a friend to drive his car into you very fast.'

But Lomper looked very sad.

'I haven't got any friends,' he said.

Dave and Gaz didn't know it, but that was Lomper's whole problem. He was shy and didn't make friends easily. He had spent the last five years looking after his mother, who was very ill. He never went out anywhere except to practise with the band and he had no real social life.

'Listen,' cried Gaz. 'We've just saved your life. So don't tell us we're not your friends, right?'

Lomper's grey eyes shone with surprise and happiness. 'Really?' he said.

'That's right,' said Dave, on Lomper's other side. 'I'll run you over with my car whenever you like.'

Lomper smiled – a big wide smile. 'Oh,' he said, happier than he had felt in months. 'Well, thanks very much, you two. Thanks a lot.'

◆

That evening, Gaz, Dave, Lomper and Nathan met in the security office of the empty factory where Lomper worked. Gaz wanted to practise dancing and this was a good place.

Gaz had told Lomper about his plan of forming a male strippers' group like the Chippendales. Lomper was so pleased to have friends that he agreed to join the group. To keep his new friends, he would agree to anything.

Gaz had asked Lomper to bring along some music. Dave was

looking through it, trying to find some sexy music they could dance to. But most of the music wasn't sexy at all — it was for bands like the factory band that Lomper played in.

'Wait a minute — what's this?' said Dave. He had found some music by the seventies group, Hot Chocolate.

'Great,' said Gaz. 'Let's hear it.'

Dave went up to the control room, and put the music on. Soon the sound of the Hot Chocolate hit, *You Sexy Thing*, filled the empty factory. Nathan, sitting uncomfortably beside Lomper, watched in horror as Gaz began to dance.

'Oh, Dad, don't, please don't!' he said, embarrassed.

But nothing could stop Gaz now. He was taking off his jacket, moving his body sexily in time to the music. A shower of money and keys fell out of the pockets, hitting Nathan and Lomper in the face. Next it was the T-shirt. But Gaz had forgotten he still

Gaz was moving his body sexily in time to the music.

19

had a cigarette in his mouth, and as he took off his T-shirt, the cigarette got caught. He began to cough and Dave quickly switched off the music.

Gaz looked around, very pleased with himself. 'Where's Nathan?' he said suddenly. But Nathan had gone.

◆

They found him much later, walking home along an empty street in Sheffield. When he heard Lomper's car stop behind him, the boy didn't even turn round.

'Nathan!' called Gaz. '*Nathan!*' But Nathan just walked on more quickly. Gaz got out of the car and ran after him.

'Why did you run off like that?' he asked his son. There was no reply so Gaz tried again. 'You're embarrassed, aren't you? You think your Dad's really stupid.'

'You're embarrassed, aren't you? You think your Dad's really stupid.'

This was exactly what Nathan was thinking and Gaz knew it. He tried to explain, to find the right words.

'Listen, Nathan. The only reason I'm doing this is because of you. I have to get enough money so that you and I can continue seeing each other. I like you, Nathan. You're my son.' He stopped, then added quietly, 'I *love* you.'

Nathan stopped walking at last and turned to face his father. Gaz pulled his son towards him and put his arms round him. 'All right, kid?' he asked softly, and Nathan smiled.

'All right, Dad,' he replied, and the two of them walked back to the car, where Lomper and Dave were waiting.

Chapter 4   Finding a Dance Teacher

The next afternoon, Gaz, Dave, Lomper and Nathan were in a most unusual place. They were sitting in a school classroom, looking down into the school hall below. There was a dancing class in the hall, and about twelve middle-aged couples were moving slowly round the floor.

It was Nathan's idea. He had seen a sign on the school notice-board advertising dancing classes. He was anxious now to help Gaz and had suggested coming to watch the class. But it wasn't the sort of dancing that Gaz was interested in.

'The notice just said "Dancing Class",' said Nathan. 'Sorry, Dad.'

'It was a great idea, kid,' replied Gaz. 'It's just not the right sort of dancing, that's all.'

'Gaz, Gaz!' Dave whispered suddenly. 'Look!'

Their old boss, Gerald Cooper, was moving smoothly across the dance floor, performing a number of complicated dance steps with his partner. Gaz began to laugh.

'He's very good, isn't he?' said Dave, his mouth open in astonishment.

21

'Yes, he is,' agreed Gaz. He stopped laughing as an idea began to form in his mind.

Just then Gerald looked up and saw the four faces looking down at him. He stopped and stared in horror, then said something to his partner. A few minutes later, the classroom door opened and Gerald stood there angrily.

'All right, you've had your entertainment. You can go home now,' he said.

Gerald hadn't expected to see anyone from the Job Club at his dancing class. It was one of the few places he felt safe, where he could forget his problems for a time.

'But you're a very good dancer, Gerald,' said Gaz.

Just then, Gerald's partner appeared behind him. Her hair was piled high on her head and she was wearing a lot of make-up and gold jewellery. This was Linda, Gerald's wife.

'Come on, Gerald, we'll miss the next dance,' she said, then stopped in surprise when she saw Gaz and the others.

Gerald was trying hard to think of something to say. He didn't want Linda to meet anyone from the Job Club. He had to get her out of there as quickly as possible. So he said the first thing that came into his head.

'Sorry, love,' he said. 'These are friends of mine ... from ... from – er – work.'

Linda stared in astonishment. These were not the kind of people she thought her husband worked with.

'Oh,' she said, then added politely, 'Are you going to join our class?'

'Well ...' Gaz was beginning, as Gerald laughed nervously and pushed Linda towards the door.

'We'd better get back now, love,' he said.

'That's right, Gerald,' said Gaz. 'You go back to your dancing class. We'll see you later.' He stopped and added with a look full of meaning, 'At work.'

Gerald turned and stared at Gaz with a look of horror. Then he left, closing the door quietly behind him.

◆

At exactly half past eight the next morning, Gaz and Dave were standing by Gerald's front gate, waiting for him to come out of the house.

Gerald's house was in a good part of town, surrounded by other houses that all looked exactly the same. They all had the same walls and the same gardens. But there was something in Gerald's garden that made it different from the others. There were plaster figures of little men placed carefully around the garden.

'He's got gnomes,' Dave said, picking up one of the brightly coloured figures. 'I don't believe it.'

'I'm not surprised,' answered Gaz. 'He and his wife are exactly the sort of people who like gnomes in their garden.'

Inside the house, Gerald was getting ready to go out. As he put his coat on, Linda handed him a pink plastic lunch box with sandwiches inside.

'Thank you, love,' said Gerald. 'I'd better go now. I mustn't be late for work.'

Gerald had lost his job at the steel factory six months ago. But he had never told his wife. He had *meant* to tell her, but it had seemed easier not to. It was easier to pretend that he still had a job. And as the weeks passed, it became more and more difficult to tell her.

Every day he left the house at eight thirty and came home at five o'clock. Linda thought he was still going to work. So she took Gerald's credit cards and went out shopping. She had just booked an expensive holiday. Gerald didn't know how to stop her spending money.

But today, for the first time in months, Gerald was feeling

more cheerful. He didn't notice Gaz and Dave until he had almost reached the gate.

'Are you going to the office?' asked Gaz with a smile.

'Yes, I am,' replied Gerald. Even Gaz couldn't spoil his good mood. He reached in his pocket, pulled out a letter and waved it in Gaz's face. 'I've got an interview for a job. It's through an old friend of mine. He owns a company and he's told me there's a job for someone like me.'

'That's great, Gerald,' said Gaz. 'But we need you to help us. We want you to teach us how to dance.'

Gerald didn't stop walking but he began to laugh.

'You two?' he said. 'Dancers? You're joking. Just look at yourselves in the mirror. You'll never be dancers. Now get out of my way, I'm busy. Don't be late for the Job Club, boys.'

He marched on and disappeared round a corner. Gaz and Dave stood looking angrily after him.

'Right,' said Gaz. 'Let's teach him a lesson.'

He turned and walked quickly back to Gerald's garden.

◆

The interview was going well, very well, Gerald thought. Three men were sitting opposite him, asking him questions and he knew the answers to all of them. He knew they were going to give him the job. It was his already.

'I'll be very glad to get back to work,' Gerald was saying. 'The last six months haven't been easy. But I've kept myself ...' He stopped, trying hard not to look at the gnome which had suddenly appeared at the window behind the men's heads, '... busy,' he managed to say at last.

'Well, you've got a very good work record, Gerald,' said the chief interviewer. But Gerald wasn't listening. He seemed to be staring at the space above the men's heads and had a look of horror on his face. The interviewer turned round, but there was nothing there. He continued, 'Er – do you really think you can do this job, Gerald?'

Two more gnomes had suddenly appeared at the window and begun to fight with each other. Gerald watched as one hit the other and broke its head. His hands began to shake.

'Oh, yes,' he whispered. 'Yes, I can do the job.'

The three men looked at each other anxiously. Gerald had seemed so good, so perfect for the job. But now they weren't sure. What was wrong with him?

◆

Later that morning, the door of the Job Club was thrown open and Gerald ran in. Gaz and Dave had never seen him so upset. His face was purple and his body was shaking with anger. He ran towards Gaz.

'It was you, wasn't it?' he shouted. 'You were moving my gnomes about at the window. You wanted my interview to go wrong. You wanted to spoil it for me.'

'What did you do it for?' he continued. 'That was my first interview in months. If I got that job, Linda would never know I lost my other one. She's in the shops now with my credit cards, spending more and more money and I can't stop her. What am I going to do now?'

He sat down, looking very sad. Gaz and Dave felt sorry for what they had done. Gerald had been their boss at work and they had never really liked him. They had always thought he was different from them. But now they realized he was in the same position as they were. Things were difficult for him too – more difficult perhaps, because Gerald was older.

'Why did you do it?' asked Gerald again. Suddenly, he was embarrassed about showing so much emotion. He didn't wait for an answer but got up, pushed past Gaz and went out.

◆

They found him later sitting on a seat in the park, feeding Linda's sandwiches to the birds and wondering what he was going to do. The four of them went up to him – Gaz, Dave, Lomper and Nathan.

'Can't you just leave me alone?' asked Gerald sadly.

Gaz was carrying a white plastic bag. He reached into it and pulled out a gnome – the same one that had been broken in the fight. Dave had stuck it back together again.

'Here's something else,' said Gaz. He reached into the bag again and brought out a little wooden cart. 'It's to say we're sorry for what we did,' he explained. 'We thought it would look nice in your garden – next to the gnomes.'

'It's really for your gnomes, not you,' said Dave, then stopped, seeing the look on Gaz's face. 'The wheels go round too,' he added quickly.

Gerald took the cart and the gnome. He couldn't really blame Gaz and Dave, he was thinking. It wasn't all their fault. He had probably lost the job already – he was too old now and had been away from work too long.

'Thanks,' he said, trying to smile. 'Thanks very much.'

'Listen, Gerald,' said Gaz. 'We're serious about needing your help. We want to learn to dance like the Chippendales. If they can do it, we can too.'

Gerald stared at Gaz in astonishment. 'But you can't dance,' he said at last.

'We know,' said Gaz. 'That's why we need your help. You're such a good dancer. Will you teach us? Please?'

Gerald thought. What had he got to lose? There would be no job offer now and there was nothing else for him to do. If Linda found out . . . but she wouldn't find out.

'All right,' he said at last. 'I'll help you.'

Chapter 5   Horse and Guy Join the Group

Gaz now had Dave, Lomper and Gerald on his side. But he knew that the group needed more people.

Gaz knew he wasn't a bad dancer himself. Lomper was very enthusiastic but his body was thin and pale and not very attractive. Gerald was good-looking and a good dancer but he was old. And Dave was the worst of all – fat and unable to keep in time when dancing.

No, the group needed someone else. Someone with a little bit of style, a little bit of magic. But how could they find such a person? They would have to advertise, like for any other job. So Gaz and Gerald put up notices on the Job Club notice-board, asking people to come to the empty steel factory next Saturday morning if they were interested.

On Saturday, Gaz, Gerald, Dave, Lomper and Nathan were sitting behind a long table in the factory, waiting. They had brought cold drinks and sandwiches with them. Nathan had borrowed Barry's cassette recorder and was sitting beside it, ready to put on the music.

Eleven o'clock came and went. One hour later, still nobody had come. The men were ready to give up and go home, when suddenly the door opened and a man came into the room.

He was black and middle-aged, and was wearing brown leather shoes, a jacket and a pale blue shirt. He didn't look like a stripper at all, thought Dave, more like a bus driver. He stood in front of them, looking down with his hands in his pockets. Gaz asked him what his name was.

'Horse,' replied the man.

'Well, Horse ... ' began Gaz, but he was interrupted by Lomper whispering something to him.

'Ask him,' Lomper said, 'why he's called Horse.'

'You ask him,' said Gaz. 'It's not because he wins races, is it?'

'He's too old,' said Gerald. 'He must be fifty at least.' Gerald himself was in his mid-fifties.

Gaz turned back to Horse. 'Well, Horse,' he said. 'What can you do?'

Horse lifted his head and thought. 'Don't know really,' he said. Gerald looked at the ceiling. This man was wasting his time. Gerald thought of all the job applications that he could be filling in.

But Horse was still speaking. He was listing the names of all the dances he could do. Some of them were very complicated and needed a lot of skill. Now everyone was listening to Horse with great interest and attention – even Gerald. His mouth fell open in astonishment.

'Show us what you can do, Horse,' said Gaz.

Nathan pressed the *Play* button and Horse began to dance. At first he moved slowly, but as he remembered the steps, he began to dance more quickly. He was really excellent, and the men watched, very surprised and pleased.

Horse had become a member of the group. He was in.

♦

The next man was a very good-looking young man in his twenties whose name was Guy and who worked as a plasterer.

'My favourite film's *Singing in the Rain*,' Guy told them. Horse had now joined them and was sitting behind the table with the others. 'There's the part where they do that "walking up the wall" thing.'

Gerald had opened a large newspaper and was hiding behind it. He didn't want Guy to see him.

'He knows me. He plastered our bathroom a few months ago,' Gerald whispered to Gaz. 'I don't want him to recognize me. Tell him to go away.'

But Gaz wasn't interested in Gerald's problems. Guy was very attractive. If he could dance well, he would be the star of their

Nathan pressed the Play button and Horse began to dance.

show and give it the magic it badly needed. 'What "walking up the wall" thing?' he asked Guy.

'I'll show you,' said Guy, jumping to his feet. He stepped back then ran at the opposite wall at full speed. He took a couple of steps up it, but then crashed to the ground and lay at the bottom, out of breath.

'Sorry. They do it better in the film,' he explained as he got up again. He tried to smile.

Clearly, thought Gaz, Guy wasn't going to be their star dancer. 'So you don't dance?' he asked the young man.

'Well – er – no,' replied Guy.

'And you don't sing?'

'No.'

'Well, then,' said Gaz, wondering why Guy had come. 'What *do* you do?'

Guy stood up and took off his clothes – first his jacket and T-shirt, then his trousers. He stood proudly before the men. Gaz, Dave, Lomper and Nathan stared in silence, admiring him. Guy had the best male body they had ever seen and the women would love him.

Gerald was still hiding behind his newspaper. At last, wondering what the others were looking at, he lowered it.

Guy knew him at once. He smiled and gave a little wave. 'Hello, Gerald,' he said, without showing any surprise. 'I didn't see you over there. I plastered his bathroom a few months ago,' he explained to the others.

'Hello, Guy,' said Gerald weakly. He too was admiring Guy's body. There was no reason to pretend any more.

With Horse's dancing and Guy's good looks, thought Gaz, their group was complete.

◆

A few days later, Gaz, Dave and Nathan were in Asda, the big new shop where Dave's wife, Jean, worked as an assistant. Gerald had told them to get some dance videos and there were plenty of videos on the shelves at Asda.

Dave could hear Jean laughing loudly. He walked towards her but then stopped. Jean hadn't seen him. She was joking and laughing with a good-looking young man called Frankie, who also worked in Asda.

Gaz saw the worried look on Dave's face. 'Don't get upset, Dave,' he told his friend. 'It's nothing serious. Jean just enjoys a good laugh, that's all.'

Dave hoped that was true. He remembered the women's conversation he had half heard when he was standing outside the toilet in the Working Men's Club. So this was the man they were talking about.

Gaz had picked up a video of the film *Flashdance*. 'This is a good one,' he said. But Gaz didn't have any money and Dave didn't either. 'Well, you know what this means,' Gaz told Dave. 'You're going to have to steal it.'

Dave looked at Gaz in horror. 'Why me?' he asked.

'Because you've got an innocent face and I haven't,' Gaz replied. He walked off with Nathan, leaving Dave standing in front of the videos.

Dave picked up *Flashdance* and put it into his pocket. Then he ran out of the main door. Immediately the shop alarm began to sound, but it was too late. Dave had escaped.

◆

Later, in Lomper's security office, the group watched *Flashdance*. The star of the film was a wonderful dancer and they watched her with open mouths, staring in astonishment at the way she moved.

'That,' Gerald said when the video ended, 'is what we're

looking for. And I'm going to teach you. Even you, Dave, will be able to dance. I'll teach you in a week.'

'Me?' said Dave. 'You're joking. I'm much too fat.'

'All right, then,' Gerald replied. 'Two weeks.'

Chapter 6   Becoming Good Friends

Dave had told Gaz many times that, although he was ready to help as much as possible, he wasn't going to take part in the final show. He was not going to take off his clothes in front of all those women. Gaz always made the same reply. Dave would have to stay in the group until they could find someone else to take his place.

So Dave stayed, but he was becoming more and more uncertain and depressed. Perhaps Gaz was lying. Perhaps he didn't intend to find anyone else at all.

He wanted to talk to Jean about it. But he didn't dare tell her he was a member of a male strippers' group. And Jean had other ideas for his future.

'They're advertising a security guard's job at Asda,' Dave told Gaz as they walked to their first dancing lesson. 'Jean thinks I should take it.'

'Security guard job?' said Gaz in horror. 'Oh, no, Dave. You're worth a lot more than that.' He knew Dave would earn very little money as a security guard.

'Jean doesn't think so,' replied Dave unhappily. He added, 'I'm sure there's something happening between her and that Frankie she works with.'

'No, Dave, you're wrong,' said Gaz. He didn't like Jean much, and she didn't like him, but he knew she was a good wife to Dave. And he had heard her say in the toilet of the Working Men's Club that she would never hurt Dave.

'Listen, Dave,' Gaz went on brightly. 'Nobody tells the

Chippendales to get jobs as security guards, do they? Think about how much money they make.'

Dave continued walking and thought about what Gaz said. It was true. He could make a lot more money dancing in the show. And Gerald had promised he would teach them all to dance within two weeks. Dave could do the show and then take the job. He knew security guards were always needed at Asda. Two weeks more wouldn't make any difference.

'Think of Jean's face when she sees you dancing,' Gaz was saying. 'Think how proud she'll be.'

Perhaps Gaz was right. For the first time in days, Dave began to feel a bit more cheerful. 'All right, Gaz,' he said. 'I'll try it.'

◆

Gerald was finding it very difficult to teach the men to dance. None of them seemed to understand what he wanted them to do. They all moved at different times, and did not look part of the same group. Lomper and Dave were the worst, but the others weren't much better.

Gerald only wanted them to dance in a straight line. 'You . . . stay still,' he said to Lomper, pushing him to one side. 'And you . . . move forwards,' he told Gaz.

Nathan had control of the cassette recorder, and when Gerald told him, he started the music again. But the men still moved at different times and finished in different positions – not in a straight line at all.

Gerald pushed his fingers through his hair. 'What do I have to do to make you understand?' he shouted.

The group stood looking at him unhappily. Lomper thought it must be his fault. He hoped Gaz wouldn't ask him to leave – these were the only friends he had. Guy was sure it was his fault because he couldn't dance. And Dave thought it was all his fault because he was too fat.

Only Horse seemed to be thinking hard. At last he said brightly, 'Well, it's like a football line-up, isn't it?'

'What?' said Gerald, feeling very tired.

Horse explained what he meant. In a football team, the players all had a certain way of moving into a straight line. Using simple football terms, Horse explained to the others what Gerald wanted them to do.

The men smiled. Now they understood completely. Why hadn't Gerald told them that before?

'Oh, well, that's easy,' said Dave.

'OK, let's try it,' said Gerald slowly, although he had no idea what Horse was talking about. 'Nathan?'

Nathan pressed the *Play* button and to Gerald's astonishment, the five men in front of him stepped forwards into one straight line in perfect time to the music.

The five men in front of him stepped forwards into one straight line in perfect time to the music.

Gerald's mouth opened and closed. 'Perfect!' he said at last. 'Perfect!'

The men smiled at each other, very pleased to have got it right at last. After that, Horse translated everything Gerald wanted them to do into simple football language. There were no more problems.

♦

The dancing lessons continued, and slowly the group began to get better. Suddenly, they had a new sense of purpose in their lives.

To his own surprise, Gaz wanted to please Gerald, to get things right. He had never felt like that when he worked for Gerald at the steel factory.

Lomper practised the dance steps secretly in his office at night. Dave kept the *Flashdance* video at home and watched it again and again while Jean was out at work.

Guy and Horse met at a video shop in the city centre, where Horse's niece, Beryl, worked. There, they watched every famous dance video that Beryl could find for them.

Gerald borrowed several *Teach Yourself Dancing* books from his local library. He lost weight and started to do exercises. For the first time in months, he felt full of life.

The group started meeting away from the dancing classes and the steel factory. Sometimes they played football in the park, or went out for a drink if they had enough money. They all stopped going to the Job Club. They didn't need it.

One wet Wednesday afternoon, the group met at Gerald's house. Gaz had said they needed somewhere private to discuss their plans, and Gerald's house was the best place. Linda was out at work.

'Come on, get inside quickly,' Gerald told them as they stood outside on his doorstep. The men came in one after the other, careful not to leave any mud on the beautiful white carpet.

Gerald's living-room was very clean and every shelf was full of Linda's things. The sofa and chairs were covered with a soft pink material and there was a glass coffee table in the centre of the room with magazines on it. In the corner of the room stood a large television.

'Put that down at once!' Gerald shouted as Dave picked up a small glass figure. Dave put it down quickly and Gerald knew he would have to check its position later. All Linda's things had special places, and she knew at once if any of them were moved.

'Right, then,' said Gaz. 'Are we ready?'

'Ready for what?' asked Horse anxiously.

'Taking our clothes off,' replied Gaz. Everyone was silent, so he went on, 'We *are* strippers, aren't we? Surely you haven't forgotten that? We've got to practise taking off our clothes.'

So this was why Gaz had got the group to come to his house, thought Gerald. He hadn't wanted to discuss things at all – he'd wanted to practise stripping. There was a look of horror on Gerald's face as he began, 'What? Here? Now? In this house? This is a good area, this is . . .' Then he stopped. Gaz had won again and Gerald knew he had lost.

Gaz wasn't listening to Gerald. He was busy taking his shirt off. Slowly, the others started to do the same. Soon they were all half-naked, looking shyly at each other's bodies. 'Now the trousers,' said Gaz, lifting his leg to take off his shoes. The others did the same.

Finally, they were all dressed only in their socks and underpants. Everyone was looking at Gerald.

'Why are you so brown?' Guy asked him.

'No special reason,' replied Gerald.

'You've got a sunbed, haven't you?' went on Guy, smiling.

'It's Linda's,' said Gerald angrily. 'And no, you can't use it. Don't even think of asking.'

Guy was going to reply when the doorbell rang. Gerald turned pale as he realized he was standing in his living-room, dressed only in his underpants and socks, with five nearly naked men.

◆

'You can't take this,' he was saying five minutes later. Two men had pushed their way into the room and were lifting up the television. There was no sign of the rest of the group.

'Oh, yes, we can,' said the bigger man. 'Our boss's orders. Sorry.'

Gerald had bought the television from a hire purchase company several months ago, when he still had a job. But since he had been unemployed, he couldn't afford to make the monthly payments on it any more. Now the boss of the hire purchase company wanted his television back. So he had sent the two men to collect it from Gerald's house.

The men picked up the television and started to walk towards the door. Suddenly, they stopped. Five men, wearing nothing except their underpants, were standing in front of them in the doorway, refusing to let them through.

'Put that down and get out of here,' said the largest man in the group.

The two men put the television down and moved quickly to the door. Their boss hadn't warned them about anything like this and they were very frightened. 'There must be a mistake,' one of them said to Gerald. 'I'll check with the office.'

They ran out of the house as fast as they could, very pleased to escape from such a terrible place. There was a big smile on Gerald's face. 'Thanks very much, everyone,' he said.

The others were crowding round Dave, congratulating him on how he had frightened the men. Dave was very happy. 'Hey, it's good fun being a stripper,' he said suddenly, and everyone began to laugh.

◆

The members of the group were forming good relationships. These six men, all so different, had become good friends. When they were at the Job Club, each man had thought only of himself and his own problems. But now dancing had made them into a team and they worked together. They asked for and gave help and advice.

Gaz's relationship with Nathan was also much better. Nathan proudly watched Gaz learning difficult dance steps, knowing his father was doing it all for him. He stopped complaining about wanting to do 'normal' things and how cold Gaz's flat was. Now he wanted to spend as much time with Gaz as possible. Gaz didn't understand the change in Nathan but he was grateful for it.

When Gaz had seen the Chippendales at the Working Men's Club, they were wearing uniforms – American firemen's uniforms, Gaz thought. So Gaz told Lomper to 'borrow' six security guard uniforms from the steel factory. They would put them back after the show, he said, so Lomper wouldn't get into trouble.

Guy's cousin owned a swimwear shop. So Guy got six red leather G-strings for the men to wear under their trousers. At first the men were embarrassed, but then they got used to wearing the G-strings as the final part of their show.

They had their music and they had their uniforms. Now it was time to fix a date and start advertising the show.

Chapter 7   Gaz Says the Wrong Thing

When he was at school, Gaz had known an older boy called Alan Rotherfield. Alan was now manager of the Millthorpe Working Men's Club – the same Club where the Chippendales had performed a few weeks ago.

Gaz went to see Alan to ask if he could hire the Club for an evening. He took Nathan along with him, hoping Alan would say yes more easily if the boy was there. Alan liked Gaz, but he was also a businessman. He wanted to be sure he wasn't going to lose any money. So he told Gaz he could hire the Club if he paid him a hundred pounds first.

'Oh, come on, Alan,' said Gaz. 'We're old friends. You know me, don't you?'

'Yes,' said Alan. 'And that's exactly why I want a hundred pounds first. Listen, Gaz. If I let you have the Club for nothing, and then you and your friends don't come, I'll be left with an empty Club on a Friday night and I'll lose a lot of business.'

'Well, of course we'll come,' said Gaz. 'And I haven't got a hundred pounds.'

'Then tell me why you want to hire the Club,' said Alan.

'I can't,' replied Gaz unhappily. 'It's a secret.'

He didn't want to tell Alan about the strippers' group. He was sure Alan would refuse to hire him the Club. But Alan was hurt that Gaz wasn't going to tell him his secret.

'All right, then, Gaz,' said Alan. 'You'll have to find the money first.'

◆

Gaz had no idea what to do next. He didn't have a hundred pounds and he didn't know who to ask.

Then Nathan suggested borrowing the money from his mother, Mandy. Gaz didn't want to ask Mandy for the money but he couldn't think of another way. So he and Nathan went to see Mandy at the clothes factory where she worked.

Mandy had done well at the factory. She had started working there when Gaz was in prison, and now she was in charge of the machine room.

Nobody took any notice of Gaz and Nathan as they walked

in. Everywhere women were working at their tables, making T-shirts and summer dresses. They didn't even look up – they were too busy with their work and listening to loud music on the radio.

From her office at the other end of the room, Mandy saw Gaz come in with her son. She hurried across the floor to meet them, wondering what they could want. Nathan should be at home doing his homework, and Gaz wasn't meant to see him until Saturday. She smiled in a loving way at Nathan.

'Hi, Mum,' said Nathan. He seemed so happy that she decided not to ask about the homework or what he was doing with Gaz. Turning to Gaz, Mandy's voice became hard. 'What do you want?' she asked him.

Gaz was wondering how he could begin. Mandy stared silently at him, waiting for a reply.

'I'm going to get you all your money,' Gaz said, smiling at her. 'I mean ... *our* money, the money for Nathan. I really am, I promise.'

'Yes, right,' said Mandy. She had heard all this before. She had spent most of her life listening to Gaz's promises, and she didn't believe them any more. 'Is that all?' she asked, still wondering what Gaz really wanted.

'Yes, I mean – er – no,' said Gaz. Suddenly, he remembered something he had seen on a poster at the Job Club. 'The problem is, Mandy ... in business, sometimes you have to put money into something to get money back.'

Mandy stepped back, her mouth opening and her eyes becoming narrow. Gaz held up his hand.

'It's all right,' he said. 'I'm going to get you the whole seven hundred pounds. I just need a little bit now.'

Mandy stared at him in astonishment.

'I don't believe I'm hearing this,' she said. 'You want *me* to give *you* some money?' She'd given Gaz so much money over the

40

years and never got it back. Now here he was, asking for more.

'Yes, that's right,' said Gaz, smiling his best smile. Nathan was smiling too, hoping she would agree.

Mandy looked at them both, then she said, 'Right. I need someone to work in the packing department. The pay's two pounds fifty pence an hour. You can start now if you like.' She stood facing them, ready to lead the way. 'Are you coming?' she asked.

The smile disappeared from Gaz's face and the light went out of his eyes. Nathan reached up and took his father's hand, gently pulling him towards the door. 'Come on, Dad,' he said softly. 'I've got an idea.'

◆

Nathan had decided to help his father as much as he could. He asked Gaz to meet him in town later that afternoon, then he went home and got his Post Office Account Book.

Nathan's parents had opened an account for him when he was a baby. They had put into it money, which he had received over the years – money from his grandparents or from jobs in the summer holidays. By now, Nathan thought, there should be over a hundred pounds in it.

As they entered the post office, Gaz realized what Nathan had in mind. 'You can't do this, kid,' he said. 'It's your money.'

'Yes, I can,' said Nathan. 'I just need your signature, that's all.' He pushed his account book towards the woman sitting behind the counter. 'I'd like to take some money out, please,' he said. 'One hundred pounds.'

But Gaz took the book out of the woman's hand. It didn't seem right to use Nathan's money to hire the Club.

'Look, Dad,' said Nathan. 'I *want* to do this. You said you'd get the money back. I know you'll pay it back to me.' He stared up at Gaz, waiting for an answer.

'I know that's what I said,' replied Gaz. 'But you shouldn't listen to what *I* say.' It was true, he knew, especially about money.

But Nathan was looking into his father's eyes. 'But you promised,' he said quietly, and paused. 'And I believe you.'

'You do?' whispered Gaz, proud and astonished at the same time. Nobody ever believed him.

'Yes,' said Nathan.

Gaz felt like crying when he saw how much Nathan loved him. He made himself a promise. Whatever happened, he would get Nathan his money back, and Mandy's too. He knew he didn't deserve a son like Nathan. He hadn't deserved Mandy either. Well, he'd lost Mandy, but there was still a chance with Nathan. A chance to make Nathan proud of him.

So he allowed Nathan to push the account book back across the counter and take out a hundred pounds.

Now they could hire the Club, and things were moving fast.

♦

The next day, Gaz visited a friend who worked in a print shop in the city centre. When he came out of the shop, he had a box of five hundred posters under his arm.

When he showed the posters to the rest of the group later, everyone was very surprised and pleased.

**MALE STRIPPERS
PRESENT**

HOT METAL

**WOMEN ONLY
MILLTHORPE WORKING MEN'S CLUB
FRIDAY 25 MAY 8.00 PM**

*The men went round the town, putting the posters up
wherever they could.*

Everyone liked the name that Gaz had chosen for the group –
Hot Metal. The men went round the town, putting the posters up
wherever they could – on bus stops, post boxes, lampposts and
fences.

All of them helped – it was a real team job. Gaz chose the
place, Lomper took out a poster and Horse and Dave held it
down while Gerald stuck it on. Guy told them if it was straight
or not. And as they put the posters up, they tried not to feel
nervous. There were only ten days until 25 May.

They were putting one up on the wall of an old pub when
two local women, Sheryl and Louise, came round the corner.
They were wearing high heels, very short tight skirts and a lot of
make-up. They walked towards the men, arm in arm and
laughing loudly. They looked very dangerous.

'Oh no,' said Gaz quietly. Both women had been his

43

girlfriends in the past. He smiled and said, 'How are you, girls?'

The two women stopped. 'Well, then, Gary,' said Sheryl. 'What are you doing?'

Louise had bright red hair and large silver earrings. She reached out and took a poster from Lomper's hand. 'What's all this about, then?' she asked in surprise, as Sheryl looked over her shoulder.

'Oh, we're just doing a bit of advertising for some friends,' said Gaz.

'Oh, yes?' said Sheryl. 'And who's going to come and see your – er – friends?' Clearly, she didn't believe that Gaz's friends existed. Then she said, 'We had the real thing here last month, you know – the Chippendales.'

'Well,' said Gaz, 'our friends are much better than the Chippendales.'

The girls laughed loudly. 'Better?' they said. 'How could they be better?'

Gaz knew he had to say something quickly and he didn't stop to think clearly. He just wanted to make some money; he wanted these women and their friends to come to the show. So he knew there would have to be something very special about the show, a reason to make them want to come. 'Well,' he said brightly. 'Our friends go all the way. They show everything.'

Sheryl and Louise couldn't believe their ears. They stared at Gaz. 'All the way?' Sheryl repeated. 'Everything? Do you mean . . . the full monty? You?'

'Yes,' Gaz said proudly.

'Well,' said Sheryl. 'That would be worth a look.' The two women moved off down the street, laughing even louder than before. 'See you there, then!'

As Gaz watched them disappear down the hill, he froze in his shoes. He could feel the surprise and anger of the rest of the group behind him. He turned round and saw their shocked faces staring at him.

'No!' Dave said. 'No, no, no! Never!'

Horse pushed forwards angrily, pointing at Gaz.

'Excuse me,' he said. 'Nobody said anything to me about the full monty.' The others agreed. The only person who didn't seem to mind was Guy. Guy knew he had a fine body and he wasn't ashamed to show it in public.

'We've got to be better than the Chippendales,' said Gaz, 'or nobody will come to see us. I couldn't think of anything else to say, to make them come to the show.'

'They know it's us, you know,' said Lomper unhappily. What would he do if his mother found out?

'Of course they know it's us,' said Gaz. 'And by the end of this evening everyone in Sheffield will know it's us, whether we do it or whether we don't.' Gerald and Dave turned pale, thinking about Linda and Jean finding out.

But Gaz hadn't finished yet. 'Listen. We can forget the whole thing and go back to the Job Club, or do it and maybe, just maybe, get rich. And I'll tell you something – people don't laugh so loudly when you've got a thousand pounds in your back pocket.'

He paused, then asked, 'Now are you in, or are you out?'

♦

The next few days weren't very happy ones. There were no more dancing practices, and the group stopped meeting completely. They were thinking about what Gaz had said. The thought of taking all their clothes off in public filled them with fear. Gerald was frightened of what Linda would say – the others were embarrassed and ashamed of their bodies. Only Guy and Gaz didn't care.

The next time they saw each other was three days later, when they were standing in the queue at the unemployment office, waiting to receive their unemployment benefit. The men stood in a line, one behind the other. Gaz, in a separate queue, was smoking a cigarette and watching them.

It wasn't really surprising that everything had gone wrong, he was thinking sadly. How could he expect the men to be strippers? They were just ordinary men, like everybody else in the queue. The strippers' group was a great idea, but it could never work.

The local radio was playing, and suddenly the Donna Summer seventies hit, *Hot Stuff,* began to play. It was a song that all the men knew well; they had danced to it many times.

From where he was standing, Gaz looked across again at the other queue. At once he noticed something different about the men he was watching. They had straightened up and were looking much brighter. Without realizing it, they all started to move their bodies in time with the music.

Gerald had reached the front of the queue. As the music got louder, he left the line and started to dance in the middle of the office floor. Behind him the others smiled. Their feet were moving backwards and forwards in perfect time.

Without realizing it, they all started to move their bodies in time with the music.

Gaz felt very happy. Now he knew the group wasn't finished – and the show would still go on.

Chapter 8   Dave Changes His Mind

As the day of the show came nearer, Dave began to get more and more worried about it.

He hated the idea of taking his clothes off in public for two reasons. First, there was his body. It was fat and ugly and made him feel embarrassed and ashamed. He knew he ate all the wrong kinds of food but he couldn't stop himself. He couldn't seem to lose any weight, and he had almost stopped caring. What reason did he have to be thin?

Then there was Jean. Things seemed to be getting worse and worse between them. He had wanted to tell her about the group and share his worries with her and ask her advice. But then he imagined the look in her eyes, and the way she would throw back her head and laugh in his face. Worse, she would tell that good-looking young man she worked with, Frankie, and everybody else down at Asda. Everyone would laugh at him, and then Jean would leave him and marry someone else.

Dave knew he had changed a lot since he lost his job. When he met Jean, he went out a lot and was very popular. Everybody liked him and he had plenty of friends. He was always going to parties and dances, and laughing and joking. That was partly why Jean had fallen in love with him. He was still fat in those days, but it hadn't seemed very important then. Now things were different.

And so Dave stayed silent, shut up in his own little world. At night, when he thought Jean was asleep, he left the house and sat in his small garden shed. There he ate chocolate and tried to think of quick ways to lose weight. He never noticed Jean watching him anxiously from the bedroom window. He never knew that she stood there crying because he didn't talk to her any more.

◆

It was time for the final practice before the show and Horse had invited his elderly mother to watch. He thought it would be a good experience for the group to dance in front of other people. His mother brought her two sisters with her. The three ladies sat in a line on an old sofa in the middle of the empty steel factory. They had no idea what to expect.

The men were changing into their security guard uniforms in a small room off the main factory floor. They were all very nervous. Nathan was there too, sitting uncomfortably on a table, ready to start the music. Suddenly, they saw a tall, very pretty girl in a short skirt and black leather boots walk across the factory floor and join Horse's mother and aunts on the sofa.

'Who's that?' asked Gerald in horror.

'That's Beryl, my niece,' replied Horse. Seeing the look of terror on Gerald's face, he added, 'It's family, isn't it? What can you do?'

None of the men looked happy or relaxed. Gaz, with a cigarette hanging from his lips, was walking up and down the room. Lomper and Guy were discussing their dance steps. Gerald was silent, worrying about the show. Horse sat with his head in his hands, trying not to feel nervous. There was only one man missing and everyone was tired of waiting.

'Where's Dave?' asked Nathan at last, saying what everyone was thinking. Gaz stopped walking up and down and turned his head. He threw down his cigarette and walked out of the door. They couldn't wait any longer – he would have to go and look for Dave.

First, he went to Dave's house, but when he knocked on the door there was no reply. Then he had an idea. Ten minutes later he had entered Asda and was walking up and down, looking right and left among the busy shoppers. Soon he saw a large man in a security guard's uniform, standing beside the sweet counter. It was Dave. But his uniform wasn't the one he was going to wear in the show. This one said *Asda* on it.

'Dave!' called Gaz. 'What are you doing?'

Dave stopped and turned to face his friend.

'What does it look like?' he said.

'The show's in three days' time. We're practising now. Where are you?'

'I'm here, working, earning some money,' said Dave. He had a strange look in his eyes. 'I've got a real job now. That's the end of the conversation, all right?' He turned and walked away.

Gaz followed him, calling his name. But Dave took no notice. He carried on walking round the shop.

Then Gaz had another idea. As he passed some jackets, he took one and held it up in front of himself. Dave turned and saw him. Then, to Dave's horror, Gaz ran towards the main door of the shop, still holding the jacket. 'Come on, then, Mr Fat Security Guard,' he shouted. 'Do your job!'

But Dave had done a lot of exercise over the past few weeks. He could run much more quickly than Gaz expected. He chased Gaz through the main door and out into the car park. Gaz turned round to look behind him and as he turned back again, ran straight into a parked car. As he fell to the ground in pain, Dave jumped on him and held him down.

'Don't ever call me fat again, all right?' Dave shouted in Gaz's face, shaking him. 'All right?' he repeated. Gaz had never seen Dave so angry. He looked up at his friend.

'Please, Dave, come back,' he said. 'We need you.' Gerald had worked out all the dances for six people. They wouldn't look right with only five. And Dave was his best friend and the one who had been with him from the start of this crazy idea. He wanted him there at the end.

49

Dave stared long and hard into Gaz's eyes, trying to control his emotions. Finally he let go of Gaz and pushed him away. 'I can't,' he said. 'I'm sorry, I just can't, all right?' Picking up the stolen jacket from the ground, he turned and walked back into Asda.

Chapter 9   In Trouble with the Police

Back at the steel factory, Horse's mother and aunts were beginning to get impatient.

'Tell them there's been a bit of a delay,' Gerald told Horse. The members of the group were disappearing – first Dave, and now Gaz.

'Well, they won't wait for ever, you know,' said Horse.

Just then the door opened and Gaz came in.

'Dave's not coming,' he told them unhappily. 'It's all right,' he continued, seeing the looks on their faces. 'We can manage without him.'

Gaz quickly changed into his security guard's uniform. A few minutes later, Nathan pressed the *Play* button on the cassette recorder and the men came out. Horse was first, then Lomper, followed by Guy, Gerald and Gaz. They formed a straight line in front of the women, and as Nathan turned up the music, began to dance.

At first the men were shy, but soon they began to enjoy themselves. They started to dance really well, watching each other carefully and keeping in time with the music. They were too busy remembering their steps to be nervous. As they danced, they took off their jackets, shirts and trousers until finally they were wearing only their red leather G-strings.

The women in front of them on the sofa watched the performance in complete astonishment. They had seen many

The women in front of them on the sofa watched the performance in complete astonishment.

unusual things in their lives, but never anything like this. They smiled at the men, enjoying every minute of the show.

Nathan too was enjoying himself, very pleased that everything was going so well. This was better than school. He turned up the music even louder. So loud that it could be heard outside the walls of the steel factory.

Usually nobody came near the empty factory. But on this day, a policeman, PC Henry, was walking round the area, checking that everything was all right. Suddenly, he stopped and listened. Wasn't that music he could hear? He knew the factory band practised there sometimes, but this was a different kind of music. It sounded like – well, seventies pop music – a Gary Glitter song. Clearly, something was happening in the factory and he had to find out more.

PC Henry walked across to the factory door, opened it carefully and looked inside. He stood there for a few minutes, unable to believe his eyes. He had been a policeman for twenty years, but this was the first time he had seen this sort of thing – and in an empty steel factory too.

Five men, almost naked, were dancing in front of a line of women. The music was so loud that at first nobody saw PC Henry. Then suddenly Guy noticed him. He stopped dancing, took hold of Lomper and ran out through a back door. Nathan stopped the music, and Gaz, Horse and Gerald all stood looking stupidly at PC Henry, not knowing what to do next.

◆

Later, at the police station, Gaz, Horse and Gerald were sitting at a table in a small office. Through the window, Gaz could see Nathan in a separate room. Two people from social services were asking him questions.

Gaz, Horse and Gerald were wearing nothing except their G-strings and thin grey blankets round their shoulders. On the other side of the table, a police inspector was sitting and writing in a notebook. 'Name?' he asked Gaz.

'Gary Schofield,' answered Gaz.

'Gerald Arthur Cooper,' whispered Gerald, trying not to say his name loudly. He was very embarrassed and upset. He'd never been arrested before in his life, he'd never even had a parking ticket. And now here he was, sitting naked in this police station like a criminal. What would happen to him? Would he go to prison? Maybe if he had a quiet word with the police inspector – but no, it was too late. His life was over.

'Name?' the inspector was asking Horse.

'Barrington Mitchell,' Horse replied. The others looked at him in surprise. What a terrible name! It wasn't surprising he preferred to be called Horse.

'And what were you doing in the steel factory?' asked the inspector.

'Stealing girders,' Gaz said at once. The others looked at him in astonishment, wondering how they ever believed in him. All of this was Gaz's fault, all of it.

The inspector clearly didn't believe him either. He said, 'Look, Gary, nobody steals girders with no clothes on.'

'We do,' said Gary brightly, 'You don't get your clothes dirty that way, do you?'

Just then, the door opened and PC Henry came in. He was holding three video cassettes in his hand. He placed them on the table in front of the inspector.

'We got these from the security camera in the factory,' he explained.

'What happened to the security guard?' asked the inspector.

'Look, Gary, nobody steals girders with no clothes on.'

The three men pulled their blankets more closely round themselves and were silent.

◆

While the others were at the police station, Lomper and Guy had jumped over about thirty garden walls and fences to reach the back garden of Lomper's house. On the way they had taken some sheets from a washing line to cover themselves. They were cold, tired and their feet hurt, but they were laughing. They hadn't had so much fun for a long time.

'Come on, Guy,' said Lomper. He had climbed up on to the roof of the kitchen which was just below his bedroom, and was standing on the top. As he held out his hand to pull Guy up behind him, the sheet fell off his shoulders, leaving him in his G-string. He hoped that none of his neighbours were at home.

At last he managed to push his bedroom window open until there was just enough space to climb through. When they were both inside, Guy and Lomper fell together on to the floor of Lomper's bedroom, still laughing.

◆

Back at the police station, an interested group of policemen and policewomen were standing in the doorway of the inspector's office, watching the video. Gaz, Gerald and Horse were watching it too, sitting uncomfortably in their blankets.

'I can't believe what I'm seeing,' the inspector said. He couldn't take his eyes off the video. He had never seen anything like it before – Gary Schofield and a group of local men performing in a strip show. And what was even more surprising – they were very good.

Gerald was watching the video closely. He too was surprised – he hadn't expected the group to be so good. They were dancing in perfect time with each other, except for one person. Gaz.

He turned and said to him, 'You're always ahead of the others.'

'No, I'm not,' said Gaz.

'Yes, you are,' said Gerald. 'Let's watch that bit again. Excuse me, can I borrow this for a moment?' he said, taking the video control from the inspector. The inspector was so surprised he couldn't speak. Gerald pressed the *Play* button again and everybody watched Gaz with interest.

'He's right,' said the inspector. 'You *are* ahead, Gaz.'

Gaz couldn't believe it. The inspector and Gerald had become friends and were discussing his dancing ability!

In the end, the police decided to let the men go. They weren't criminals and they hadn't broken into the steel factory. And the boy seemed to be all right.

While he was putting his clothes on, Gaz tried to see Nathan. But he was stopped by a police officer.

'What do you mean, I can't see him?' asked Gaz angrily. 'He's my son.'

'Sorry,' said the police officer. 'You'll have to make an appointment with social services.'

Suddenly, the door of the police station opened and Mandy rushed in. The police had telephoned her at work, and told her Nathan wasn't at school. Instead, they said, he was at the steel factory, watching five half-naked men dance.

Mandy had come at once. She was very angry with Gaz. So this was his great money-making plan – leading Nathan into bad ways. What did he think he was doing? Or was it all her fault? Why hadn't she lent him the hundred pounds? And what would Barry say?

Nathan appeared, wearing a policeman's hat. He smiled at his father, then saw his mother and ran over to her. 'Hi, Mum,' he said.

'Oh, Nathan,' Mandy said, very pleased to see he was all right. 'Come on, we're going home.'

Gaz stepped forward. He'd done nothing wrong and he wanted Mandy to understand that. He didn't like the look in her eyes. She had never looked at him like that before. 'I can explain everything, Mandy,' he said.

Mandy turned to him angrily.

'Look, Gaz. You're unemployed and you've got to give me seven hundred pounds. And now you get arrested and finish in a police station. Do you still think you're a good father for Nathan?'

'He *is* trying, Mum,' said Nathan quietly.

But Mandy hadn't finished. 'It's too late,' she said, as Gaz tried to put his jeans on. 'Just look at yourself, Gaz.' She went out, taking her son with her.

◆

Gerald turned the corner into the street where he lived. It had been the second worst day of his life. The first had been when he lost his job.

He saw a large van parked outside his house. Two men – the same two men from the hire purchase company – were carrying furniture and other things out of his house and putting them into the van. Gerald started to run towards them in horror. Then he saw Linda standing on the doorstep, holding one of the garden gnomes.

'All right, then?' one of the men called nervously to Gerald, hoping that Gerald was alone this time.

Gerald walked slowly up to his wife and looked into her eyes. He could see there was no hope for him.

'How long have you been unemployed?' she asked.

'Well – er – about six months,' replied Gerald. Then he was silent, not knowing how to explain.

Linda didn't speak for several minutes. Then she said, 'I can manage without the sunbed, the car, the television. But six months! And you didn't tell me . . . your wife!'

She held up the gnome and threw it on the ground. It lay there, broken into hundreds of pieces.

'I thought you liked them,' said Gerald sadly.

Linda looked at him angrily. 'No, Gerald,' she said, 'I never liked them.'

Chapter 10   Problems

Gaz was lying on the sofa in his cold flat, smoking and feeling very sorry for himself. He was thinking about Mandy and what had happened at the police station.

Somewhere deep inside him, Gaz had always hoped he still had a chance with Mandy. He wanted her to leave Barry and come back to him, so he and Mandy and Nathan could be a happy family again.

He had never really loved anyone except Mandy. He knew she didn't love that boring Barry. How could she, when she had once loved Gaz so much?

But at the police station, for the first time, Gaz had realized that everything was over. The look in her eyes told him Mandy wasn't in love with him any more. And if that were true, it meant she was serious about the money. If he couldn't pay her the seven hundred pounds, she would take Nathan away from him and he would never see him again. That thought was very painful for Gaz.

Suddenly, there was a ring at the doorbell. Gaz jumped up, putting out his cigarette. Perhaps it was Mandy come to say she was sorry and bringing Nathan with her.

But it wasn't Mandy. It was Gerald standing on the doorstep. Linda had told him to leave and so he had thrown some things into a bag and come to see Gaz, hoping he could stay with him for a few days. He was free of his wife for the first time in thirty-two years.

Gerald had some other news as well. He took a letter out of his pocket and waved it at Gaz. 'Guess what?' he said. Gaz couldn't imagine what was in the letter, so Gerald continued, 'They've offered me that job.'

'Congratulations,' said Gaz.

Gaz talked about his problems with Gerald and decided he was going to fight for Nathan, to win him back. He wasn't going to let Mandy and Barry take control of his son.

◆

The next day, Gaz and Gerald went to meet Nathan after school. Nathan was happy to see his father, and smiled and waved hello.

'Do you want to play football in the park?' asked Gaz.

But before Nathan could reply, he heard his mother's voice and saw Mandy and Barry hurrying towards him. Barry's new car was parked further down the street.

'Nathan!' called Mandy. She put her arm round her son and told Gaz angrily, 'You shouldn't even be here!'

Gaz knew what she meant. That morning he had received a letter from the court, warning him to stay away from Nathan. They had heard about his arrest from the people at social services.

Nathan looked sadly at his father. 'We're going swimming, Dad. Do you want to come?'

Gaz looked from Mandy to Barry and then back to Nathan. 'I can't, kid,' he said.

'Why not?' asked Nathan.

'I just . . . can't,' Gaz whispered. 'Sorry.' He felt hot tears in his eyes.

Nathan turned to his mother. 'I understand,' he said. 'He's not allowed to, is he?'

Mandy was almost crying herself. She had once loved Gaz very much. Why wasn't there another way of doing things? She took her son's hand and said, 'Come on, Nathan.' Then she led him back to Barry's car, still trying to control her emotions. Barry followed behind.

Gerald had watched everything and had seen how upset Gaz was. He didn't say a word, but put his arm round Gaz's shoulders as Barry's car disappeared down the street.

◆

Dave was walking round Asda in his security guard's uniform for the twentieth time that morning. His feet hurt and he was very bored. Why didn't someone steal something? If they did, he would have something to do.

'Dave!' whispered a voice. 'Hey, Dave!'

It was Gaz.

'What do you want?' Dave asked him coldly. He hoped Gaz wasn't going to try and trick him into joining the group again. 'I told you before. I've finished with it.'

'We've all finished with it, Dave,' said Gaz unhappily, remembering what had happened in the police station. Dave knew about this too – Gerald had come and told him. Gerald had also told him about Gaz's problems with Nathan. Dave was very sorry for Gaz, and his voice became kinder.

'I'm sorry about Nathan,' he said, starting to walk beside Gaz. But Gaz had come to give Dave some other news.

'I've come to tell you about Lomper,' he said. 'His mother died a few days ago.'

'Oh, I'm sorry,' said Dave again. He knew how much Lomper's mother meant to him. Lomper had looked after her for years – he had done everything from cooking to giving her baths.

Dave watched Gaz's face and waited. He knew Gaz wanted something more.

'Dave,' said Gaz. 'Could you get me a jacket for the funeral?'

'Gaz . . .' began Dave.

'It's not for me, it's for the funeral,' said Gaz. 'I'll put it back afterwards.'

Dave looked over his shoulder carefully. 'What colour?' he asked.

'Orange . . . what colour do you think? Black, of course. It's for a funeral, you fool,' said Gaz impatiently, wondering why Dave was so stupid sometimes.

'Well, all right,' said Dave. 'Look, meet me by the main door in five minutes' time.'

Gaz walked slowly over to the door and waited. A few minutes later, Dave walked towards him carrying not one, but two black jackets. He held one of them out to Gaz.

'Why have you brought two?' asked Gaz.

'Because I'm coming to the funeral with you,' replied Dave. 'I'm not working in this place any more. I'm going crazy here. Ready?'

'Ready when you are,' said Gaz. He was pleased and surprised that Dave was coming with him. The two men marched side by side through the doors and across the car park. They hadn't got very far when every alarm in Asda started to sound. They increased their speed to a run, free again and shouting as loudly as they could.

♦

A reporter from the local newspaper, the *Sheffield Star*, had heard about the men's arrest and the story was on the front page of the paper. Suddenly, the group found themselves the subjects of a lot of local – and unwelcome – interest.

They were recognized everywhere they went – Guy when he was out running, and Horse when he was collecting his unemployment benefit. They had to accept it – they were becoming famous. People were interested and very amused.

Gerald wasn't happy about this at all. He didn't want anyone to recognize him, or to know he was part of a male strippers' group. So he went round the newspaper shops, buying as many copies of the *Sheffield Star* as he could. It cost him a lot of money, and he put them all in the plastic rubbish buckets in the street. The local shop owners all thought he was very strange.

Lomper was feeling very sad after his mother's death, but also glad that he now had friends to give him support. He still played his cornet in the factory band. The band were playing in a school concert the following week, and Lomper went along to the practice.

But the other members of the factory band had read the *Sheffield Star*. Without saying anything to Lomper, they decided to play a joke on him. Just as Lomper was getting ready to play his cornet, the men around him started to play something different. Lomper thought he had made a mistake. Then, to his astonishment, he recognized what they were playing – the opening part of *The Stripper*.

He put down his cornet and smiled shyly, listening and enjoying the joke as much as they were. His secret was out.

Chapter 11 The Full Monty

It was the morning of Friday 25 May. Gaz was walking down the street on his way to see Alan, the manager of the Millthorpe Working Men's Club. He had a difficult job to do and he wasn't looking forward to it. He had to tell Alan that they weren't going to do the show.

Worse, he had to ask Alan for his hundred pounds back. That was Nathan's money, not his. He had been a fool to let Nathan take it out of his post office account.

Perhaps, thought Gaz, he would have to take that job in

Mandy's clothes factory. Then she could see he was trying to do something.

As Gaz crossed the street, a car stopped beside him and a man jumped out. It was Alan. He stood in front of Gaz, waving his arms excitedly. 'Where have you been?' he said. 'I've been looking everywhere for you. I haven't heard from you in days.'

Gaz stared at Alan unhappily. Then he said, 'We're not doing it, Alan. The show's off. Sorry.'

'You must be joking,' said Alan, 'You've got to do the show. I've sold two hundred tickets.'

Gaz froze, his heart in his mouth. 'How many?' he said. He was silent, trying to work out how much money they would get for two hundred tickets.

◆

Guy, Horse and Lomper were sitting at a table in the Job Club, feeling very sorry for themselves. They were back to their old way of life, filling in job applications and playing cards. Dave was sitting at a computer, trying to type a letter and feeling very depressed. Why hadn't he stayed at Asda? Everything was Gaz's fault. Everything.

The door opened and Gerald walked in, wearing a new grey suit and with a big smile on his face. Luke Marcus, the Job Club manager, hurried over to meet him. Gerald was a big success story for the Job Club. Although he was fifty-three, he was back at work within six months. He was a wonderful example for the others.

'Congratulations, Gerald,' said Luke. 'Well done!'

Gerald had wanted to come and say goodbye to his friends, but now he felt a little embarrassed. He was very pleased to have a job, but he knew he would miss them. They had had a lot of fun together.

'Nice suit, Gerald,' said Horse.

'You never know,' Gerald told them. 'There may be jobs for you too. I'll see what I can do.'

He turned towards the door, but before he could go, Gaz appeared. He looked like a different person. His eyes were shining brightly and he had a look on his face which Dave didn't like. It was a look that usually meant trouble.

'All right, Gaz?' asked Guy, wondering, like the others, why Gaz looked so cheerful.

'We're on!' shouted Gaz. 'We're doing the show tonight! We've sold two hundred tickets.'

'What?' said the others, surprised and very pleased.

'Two hundred tickets – two thousand pounds!' said Gaz. It had taken him a long time to do the sum.

Gerald interrupted him. 'Oh, it's a bit late for all that now, Gaz.' He showed Gaz his new suit. 'I mean . . . I mean, it's a new start for me.'

Gaz looked at Gerald with fire in his eyes. 'Come on, Gerald, do it one more time. You can wear a suit for the rest of your life,' he said.

'Yes, come on, Gerald,' said the others.

Gerald thought about what Gaz had said. It was true. He had the rest of his life to wear a suit. Tonight was his chance to have fun. There was no Linda, no neighbours to worry about. He had grown very fond of these men and he had to help them. So he said, 'All right, then. I'll do it. Just once.'

Gaz turned to Dave. 'You too, Dave?' he asked softly.

Dave wished he could be like Gerald and join in the fun. But he was too embarrassed. So he pretended he didn't want anything to do with the show.

'Sorry, I can't,' he said, and turned back to the computer, trying to hide the sadness in his eyes.

◆

Dave left the Job Club twenty minutes later and went home. He didn't want to listen to the others talking excitedly about their plans for the evening.

He turned the key of his front door and stepped inside. To his surprise there was a small suitcase in the hall. What could it mean? Was Jean going somewhere? Perhaps her mother was ill. He hoped it wasn't bad news. 'Jean?' he called. 'Jean?'

He climbed the stairs to their bedroom and found Jean sitting on the bed with her jacket on. She had her back to him. Dave knew there was something very wrong. He sat down on the bed next to her.

'What's the matter, Jean?' he asked gently.

Jean turned to face him and he saw that her face was wet with tears. She was holding Dave's red leather G-string in her hand. She had found it at the back of a drawer when she was putting away his socks.

'Well, this explains a few things,' she said. 'All those nights you were late home. I thought you were out looking for a job. I've been so stupid. You were with another woman, weren't you?'

'No, Jean, no. I was with Gaz . . . really,' said Dave.

'Oh, I see,' said Jean. 'She's one of Gaz's girlfriends, is she? That makes it even worse.'

Jean had never liked Gaz. She had tried many times to keep Dave away from him, afraid that he would lead Dave into trouble.

She began to hit Dave. He stood up, held her shoulders and said, 'Just listen, will you? There's no other woman. I'm . . . I was a stripper, right? Me and Gaz and some others thought we could make a bit of money by taking our clothes off. The G-strings were for our show.'

Jean stopped crying and was silent, listening. She stared at Dave in astonishment. She hadn't expected to hear this.

'Strippers?' she repeated. 'You – and Gaz – strippers?' She couldn't believe it.

'Yes,' said Dave. 'We were quite good.' Jean waited for him to continue, but he looked down, embarrassed. 'But . . . in the end I couldn't do the show.'

'Why not, Dave?' Jean asked.

'Because I'm too fat,' Dave replied sadly. 'Look at me, Jean. Who wants to come and see me dance?'

Jean put her arms round her husband. So this was what his problem of the past few months was all about. He was unhappy because of his weight, because he was fat. She looked up into his face, her eyes shining with love. 'Me, Dave.' she said. 'I do.'

♦

The Millthorpe Working Men's Club was full of women, smoking, drinking and laughing excitedly. Worse than that for Gaz, there were at least fifty men. Men from the pub, from Lomper's factory band – even the police were there.

'It's for women only!' Gaz complained to Alan.

'Nobody told me,' Alan lied. 'I didn't know.' He wasn't going to turn away the men and lose a lot of money. The Club had never been so full, not even for the Chippendales. There must be four hundred people out there.

The men were in a small dressing room at the back, putting on their uniforms. To everyone's surprise, Gaz was the most nervous of all. He couldn't keep still – he was walking up and down the room.

'You'll be all right when you're on stage,' said Gerald, fixing the top button of his shirt.

'On stage?' repeated Gaz in horror. 'I'm not going anywhere near the stage. I'm not going out there!'

Just then the door opened and Dave came in, dressed in his uniform, smiling and ready for the show.

'Dave!' cried the others in astonishment. Everyone was very pleased to see him. Dave's eyes were shining with happiness and he looked like a different man. Nathan followed him into the room.

'There was nothing on television tonight,' Dave joked, 'so I thought I'd come and join you. I found Nathan walking around outside.'

Gaz looked angrily at his son. Mandy would kill him if she found out he was here.

'It's all right, Dad,' said Nathan. 'Mum's out front in the crowd.'

'Is she?' said Gaz in astonishment. 'With Barry?'

'No, she didn't let him come. She said it was for women only,' said Nathan, knowing his Dad would be pleased.

Alan rushed in again. The crowd was getting impatient, he told them. They'd paid their money and they didn't want to wait any longer. 'I can't keep them quiet,' he said. 'You'll have to go on now.'

Suddenly, Dave became the leader of the group. 'Get your jackets on,' he told the others, then stepped out on to the stage and began to speak. Looking out into the darkness, he could see Jean sitting with her friends, Sharon and Bee. She was smiling at him, proud and happy.

'We may not be young,' Dave told the crowd. 'We may not be pretty. But we're here . . . and for one night only, we're going for the full monty.'

The crowd cheered loudly as the rest of the men followed Dave out on to the stage and lined up behind him. Then the stage lights went on and the music began to play.

Gaz sat alone in the dressing room. Mandy was looking for him on the stage, wondering where he was. Perhaps he came on later.

Nathan decided it was time for him to do something. 'I'm going to get really angry with you in a minute, Dad,' said Nathan. He put the security guard's hat on Gaz's head. 'Listen, do you hear that noise? All those people cheering? Well, *you* did that.

'They're cheering for you. Now get out there with the others . . .'

They're cheering for you. Now get out there with the others . . . now. Go on! Out!' He held up his arm and pointed towards the door.

Gaz was very surprised but he was also grateful to Nathan. He knew he had no choice – he had to do the show. When the crowd saw him join the others on the stage, another enormous cheer went up.

The men were dancing really well, moving their bodies sexily in perfect time to the music. Not one of them was nervous now. This was their big moment and they were enjoying themselves very much. The crowd was loving every minute of the performance – even the police were cheering.

Gerald saw Horse's pretty niece, Beryl, and smiled at her warmly. He wondered if she would be interested in an old man like him. Like the others, he felt like a different person.

The men were dancing really well, moving their bodies sexily in perfect time to the music.

Tonight was the end of a long and difficult journey for them all – Gaz, Dave, Gerald, Horse, Lomper and Guy. It hadn't been easy but they had done it.

Gerald had a new job and was free of Linda at last. Dave's troubles with Jean were at an end and they could start again. Gaz, the proud father of Nathan, would soon have enough money to give Mandy, and maybe, just maybe, win her back. Lomper had made new friends and had had a lot of fun. Everyone had changed a lot over the past weeks as they found there was a lot more to life than the Job Club.

The men took off their jackets, shirts and trousers and, smiling, threw them into the excited crowd. Finally, they were naked except for their red leather G-strings. They turned their backs to the crowd and the G-strings fell to the floor.

The men took off their jackets, shirts and trousers . . .

. . . and, smiling, threw them into the excited crowd.

Then, while everyone went crazy with cheering, they turned round again, holding only their hats in front of them. They smiled happily, threw their hats in the air and stood in front of the crowd, naked and proud.

ACTIVITIES

Chapters 1–2

Before you read

1 What do you know about this story? Have you seen the film? If not, what have you heard about it?

2 Find these words in your dictionary. They are all in the story.

application   astonish   band   canal   cornet   depressed girder   naked   queue   security guard   steel   strip

a Match some of the words with the correct meaning.

a musical instrument   to surprise (someone)

a group of musicians   to undress

a line of people   with no clothes on

a metal   very, very sad

b Complete the sentences.

The steel ..... is too heavy for me to lift.

The manager of the company asked me to fill in an ..... form.

The ..... ran after the thief and caught him.

In the past, more boats travelled along the ..... .

After you read.

3 Answer the questions.

a How has Sheffield changed in the last twenty-five years? Why has it changed?

b Why is Gaz angry about the Chippendales at first? Why does he change his mind?

c Why do the men feel the Job Club is not helpful?

4 Which of the people in the story:

a is worried about her husband?

b has a lot of crazy ideas?

c was a manager at the steel factory?

d wants his father to do normal things?

e falls into the canal and gets his clothes wet?

f tries to help unemployed people find jobs?

Chapters 3–4

Before you read

5 What do you think Gaz's idea is? Will Dave want to help him? Why/why not?

6 Find these words in your dictionary.

cart credit card gnome horror kid plaster

   a Which word describes:

   an emotion?   a vehicle?

   a child or young person?   a form of money?

   b What meanings does *plaster* have in your language?

   c What kind of person buys *gnomes* for their garden, in your country?

After you read

7 Who is speaking? Who are they talking to?

   a 'I can't swim.'

   b 'Are you going to join our class?'

   c 'Oh, Dad, don't, please don't!'

   d 'Can't you just leave me alone?'

   e 'Let's teach him a lesson.'

8 Are these sentences true or false? Correct the false ones.

   a Dave stops Lomper killing himself.

   b Gerald goes to work each day.

   c Gaz is allowed to see Nathan once every two weeks.

   d Mandy and Barry are married.

   e Gaz has spent time in prison for stealing cars.

   f Gaz and Dave are surprised that Gerald is a good dancer.

Chapters 5–6

Before you read

9 What do you think Gerald's wife, Linda, will say if she finds out that Gerald has lost his job?

10 What kind of relationship do these couples have?

   a Gerald and Linda   c Gaz and Mandy

   b Dave and Jean

11 Check these words in your dictionary.

alarm   G-string   hire purchase   underpants   worth

   a Which do people wear?

   b Which do you hear?

   c Which is a form of payment?

   d Which has a similar meaning to *value*?

After you read

12 What qualities does Gaz think Horse and Guy will bring to the group?

13 Describe each of these people in one sentence:

   Horse   Guy   Lomper   Gerald   Dave

14 What importance do these have in the story?

   a the video *Flashdance*

   b the language used in a football match

   c the supermarket Asda

   d the film *Singing in the Rain*

Chapters 7–8

Before you read

15 Imagine you are Gaz. How will you advertise the show to the local women?

16 Can you think of a good name for the group?

17 Answer the questions. Find the words in *italics* in your dictionary.

   a Where can you open an *account*?

   b Who pays *benefit*?

   c What is a *poster* for?

   d What do people keep in a garden *shed*?

After you read

18 Discuss these questions.

   a Why doesn't Gaz want to tell Alan the reason for hiring the Working Men's Club?

   b Why doesn't Gaz want to take the job in Mandy's clothes factory?

   c Why is Dave worried about taking part in the show?

19 Who are these people? What is their part in the story?

   a Beryl   **c** Alan Rotherfield

   b Sheryl and Louise   **d** Frankie

Chapters 9–11

Before you read

20 Dave has said he won't take part in the show. Can you think of any reason to make him change his mind?

21 Answer the questions. Check the meanings of the words in *italics*.
  a What usually happens after someone is *arrested*?
  b When might people *cheer*?
  c Where do *funerals* take place in your country?

After you read

22 Work in pairs. Act out this telephone conversation.
  Student A: You are Linda. You are very angry. Telephone the owner of the hire purchase company. Ask him why he has sent his men to take away your things.
  Student B: You are the owner of the hire purchase company. Explain why you want your things back. Tell Linda what happened when you sent men to her house to take away the television.

23 Answer the questions.
  a How does Dave become a different person after his conversation with Jean?
  b Why doesn't Gaz want to go on stage? How does Nathan make him change his mind?
  c How have each of the men changed since they formed the strippers' group?

Writing

24 Imagine you are a reporter working on the *Sheffield Star*. Write about the show for the paper's front page.

25 Imagine you are the police inspector who interviewed Gaz, Horse and Gerald. Write a report of the interview.

26 Choose two men from the group. Compare their situations and describe how they change.

27 Imagine the next meeting between Gaz and Mandy or Linda and Gerald. Write about what happens.

28 What do we learn from *The Full Monty* about Sheffield and its people?

29 In some ways *The Full Monty* was a very unusual film. Why do you think it was so successful?